For Pepper and Tuna.

Inspired by Almarie Vitale

In a grand oak tree, there once lived two beautiful butterflies named Beth and Barry.

Beth and Barry had a tiny baby caterpillar named Bob. They were a very HAPPY family.

One day, Barry was collecting food for his family when he saw a SCARED baby caterpillar who was all alone.

He was about to be eaten up by a hungry bird!

Barry saved the baby caterpillar by flying into the eyes of the bird SCARING him away.

Barry was EXCITED to take the baby caterpillar home to raise him as part of his own family.

They named the little guy Marty. He was a different species but the family welcomed Marty with open wings.

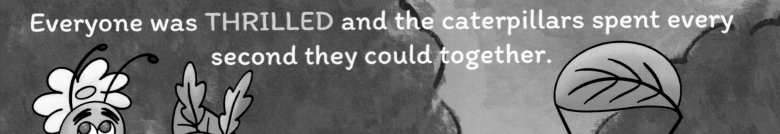

Everyone was THRILLED and the caterpillars spent every second they could together.

The day arrived when it was time for Bob to form a chrysalis.
He wanted to learn how to fly just like his mom and dad.
Bob carefully created his chrysalis and now
it was time to wait PATIENTLY.

BOB

The next day it was time for Marty to make his cocoon so he could learn how to fly too! It would take between 5 and 21 days before they are ready to emerge.

Marty knew he was different and was ANXIOUS
to see what he would look like!

They were both ready to emerge at the same time- as if they couldn't stand being apart for too long.

When Bob and Marty hatched, Bob came out as a beautiful sparkling butterfly and Marty was a fuzzy white moth.

ECSTATIC, the boys went to test out their new wings. They flew over to a crystal blue lake to view their reflections.

Marty took a look at his reflection and SADLY turned to Bob.
"Why do you look so colorful and I am so blank?" asked Marty, sounding very disappointed.
To cheer Marty up, Bob declared, "You look great!"

Still DISSATISFIED, Marty said, "That's no fair, I am going to fix it. You look so pretty and colorful and I look so boring. Why do I have to look different?"

"I don't know, but I will help you. We can figure this out together," Said Bob.

Across the lake they saw a couple having a picnic with a pitcher of red fruit punch.

Marty flew right towards the fruit punch. He tried to dive in, but the people were ANNOYED and swatted him away.

Bob felt RELIEVED when he saw a bunch of squashed berries on the floor. He suggested, "why don't you roll around in those and maybe the color will rub off."

"Good idea!" exclaimed Marty, as he went right for it.

This worked at first...

But when it began to rain, the color washed right off.

The next day they tried again.

This time, Marty decided to rub himself on a freshly painted wall, hoping that would give him some color.

But the paint dried on him, and Marty struggled to move.

He fell and the dry cracked paint flaked right off his wings.

DEVASTATED, Marty flew off to be alone and think.

Bob flew home to inform their parents that Marty flew away.

"Marty was really upset and said he needed time to think," Bob explained in a panic.

WORRIED, his family went searching for Marty.

All of a sudden, a man with a huge butterfly net saw the most amazing butterfly wings he had ever seen!

He decided to capture the butterfly family for his collection.

Luckily, the man didn't notice Marty's simple wings.

But Marty noticed his family's capture.

Marty screamed at the top of his lungs, "That's my family!"

He BRAVELY flapped his wings as hard as he could, aiming right at the man's eyes.

FRIGHTENED, the man dropped the net and ran away, as Marty's butterfly family escaped from the huge butterfly net.

The family graciously thanked Marty and told him,
"See you are perfect, just the way that you are."

Beth and Barry said, "You are our hero! We are so PROUD of you and we love you always." Barry the Butterfly then told him, "Always remember that you are beautiful just the way you are!"

"I LOVE my beautiful wings just the way they are! I don't need to change. I LOVE myself just the way I am." said Marty.